TWISTED PERSONALITIES
ANOTHER JULIA LILLUS CRIME THRILLER

JAMES ROBERTS

Edited by
JAMES ROBERTS
Illustrated by
JAMES ROBERTS

CONTENTS

INTRODUCTION

This book is a work of fiction and continues with the other Julia Lillus Series of Crime Thrillers by James Roberts.

"She cannot stay away from the bed with men, and he, the drama artist, perfects the horror of torture."

MISSING PERSONS

A fter another big day,
Julia and Richard pull into the Harford Police Department
parking lot and walk exhaustingly to the entrance. As soon as Julia
enters the reception area, Betsy runs up to her.

"Julia, I just received a phone call from a Mrs. Samuels. She says
her husband has been missing for two days and would like our help in
finding him."

"Oh, Betsy, not another missing person. I am so tired and not
ready for another missing person."

"I am so sorry, Julia. I did tell her to wait until you returned."

"That's OK, Betsy. I will look into it as soon as I get the reports
finished for this recent case."

"Julia, do you think this case will be another bizarre matter?" asks
Richard.

"Heaven knows, Richard. You have had a big day today, so as soon
as Bobbie and Amanda return, take your wife home. I can finish out
the day. Go and enjoy your little ones."

"OK, Julia, I will be in bright and early tomorrow morning to
tackle this missing person."

"Hi honey, I stopped at the grocery to pick up your favorite meal fixings. I will be home shortly. I love you."

"Mark, I love you too. Thanks for thinking about me. I can't wait to see you. Let's do something special tonight."

"OK, Samantha, I can't wait to see you either. Bye, sweetheart."

Mark finishes his conversation with his wife Samantha; a hand covers his mouth from behind, and he is forced into a van.

"What! Who are you, and why am I here?" asks Mark.

"Shut up! You will find out soon."

"Hey John, how are you coming with your stage props and costumes?" asks Bill McMasters.

"No problems yet. Thanks so much, Mr. McMasters, for letting me use this room for my work."

"John, it is no problem. This old high school used to be a bustling place. At least some of it can be used and for good use as well. Your degree studies in drama requires a place for yourself I am assuming? I will be going out of town for a few weeks. Are you going to need anything from me before I leave?" asks Mr. McMasters.

"No, sir, I will be OK. Have a great trip, and we can catch up with each other when you get back," says John.

THE BASEMENT

Mark wakes up from being drugged when kidnapped and forced into the van. As he looks around at his surroundings, he notices the room he is in, is a basement, and his hands and feet shackled to a student's type of desk he is sitting in.

"Hey! Hey! Where the hell am I?" asks Mark with a yell.

There is no response. Mark continues to yell in hopes that someone will hear him.

Suddenly there is a sound coming from the top of the stairs leading down to the basement.

"Hey! What am I doing here, and why am I tied to this desk?" asks Mark angrily.

Mark notices the noise he is hearing becomes a visual of a hobo descending the stairway; at least that is what the figure looks like by the way he/she appears. The hobo looks at Mark and smiles while raising his hand in a wave. He skips over to a record player and places a record onto the turntable. As he puts the needle onto the recording and starts it spinning, the tune "Twinkle, Twinkle Little Star" is heard.

"Who the hell are you?" asks Mark.

"We are going to have fun. Let me show you how I can juggle," says the hobo.

"Who the hell are you and what do you want with me. Why am I tied up?"

"Don't be rude, John. You are ruining my show. Don't you enjoy it?"

"My name is not John. My name is Mark. Who is this, John?"

"Watch this. I can pull a handkerchief from my buttonhole."

"I don't want to see more tricks. Untie me and let me go. My name is Mark, and my wife is waiting for me."

A cell phone starts ringing, and the hobo walks over to a box and pulls the phone out.

"Hey John, the call is a Samantha. Is she your wife, John?"

"Let me answer it, you bastard!"

"I don't think your hubby wants to talk to you," the hobo says without answering the phone and pushes the button releasing the call.

"Let me talk to her!"

"No, John, you can't talk to her, but if you would like me to give a message to her for you…"

"Don't you dare touch my wife! So help me if you even put one finger on her. I swear I will kill you!"

"Kind of hard to do being all tied up, isn't it?" asks the hobo as he slams his hand across Mark's face causing instance redness to his cheek.

"Barbara, I have been trying to call Mark, and he isn't answering," says Samantha.

"Maybe he had to work late," says Barbara.

"No, he had called me from the grocery store, and he was on his way home. It has been an hour since I talked to him on my phone. I have called several times, and he isn't answering his phone. I am worried."

"Samantha, why don't you come on over and we can have tea while waiting for Mark to return," says Barbara.

———

The hobo ascends the basement stairway and closes the door behind him. Mark finds himself alone and tries to devise a plan to get loose from the ropes tying his hands to the desk.

Mark's cellphone starts ringing from the box where the hobo put it.

"Samantha honey, I am sorry I can't get to the phone. Someone is holding me hostage. I am so sorry...."

The door to the stairway leading to the basement opens, and Mark sees a man descending dressed in a suit and tie with a briefcase in hand.

"John, my name is Marty, and I am the lawyer for your case."

"I told you. My name is not John. My name is Mark, Mark Samuels."

"John, we have a very tough case, here, with the murders and all."

"What murders? Who the hell are you? I told you my name is not John, you bastard!"

"Look, John, you need to tell the authorities where you hid the bodies of those girls you murdered. It is not going to go good for you unless you tell them. You can tell me, and I will do my best to get the best deal for you. If you don't cooperate...well, you will be headed for a death sentence."

"I, I, don't know who you are, and I did not murder anyone! You must be mistaken."

"Shut up! I didn't tell you to talk to me," says the lawyer as he places his fist, hard, on Mark's face causing a welt above his eye and an immediate bruise on his cheek.

Mark shakes his head in pain as the lawyer ascends the stairway of the basement with the door closing behind him.

"Barbara, I am anxious about Mark."

"Here, Samantha, share some tea with me. Let's see if we can sort this out. Samantha, do you think maybe Mark is having an affair?"

"Well, Barbara, I am beginning to think so… It appears he might be. Why would he do that to me? What did I ever do to deserve this?"

"Oh, Samantha, do you really think he is cheating on you?"

Mark cannot get the rope bindings loose enough to free his hands. He bows his head to his arms and closes his eyes. Suddenly, he senses someone staring at him, and he immediately opens his eyes as he raises his head.

"Who are you?" asks Mark.

"I am an empty shell of a man. You see, John, when I was young, my father left my mother, and she got hooked up with a nasty boyfriend. He didn't like me. My sister and I were very close; she was only fourteen years old. One night when my mother's boyfriend came home, he was drunk. He beat my mother and hit me several times across my face. I was so scared. I ran to my sister's bedroom and grabbed a blanket to sleep on the floor. Sometime during the night, he came in and, with his belt, tied my hands behind my back. He went over to where my sister was lying on the bed and unzipped his pants. He placed his hand over her mouth while yanking her panties down her legs. He laid on top of her, and he placed himself into her crotch. He raped my sister, and I couldn't do anything to help her," says the man in front of Mark as tears run down his cheeks.

"Are you, John? I feel your pain, and I am so sorry for your sister," says Mark.

"John, why didn't you help your sister?" asks the man.

"My name is Mark Samuels. I told you that. I have an empty soul too. I am a nobody. Now please release me. Please let me go. My wife is waiting for me."

The man walks away and ascends the basement stairs.

Mark, perplexed to what is going on, tries to think how to outsmart this guy and get loose.

The door to the basement opens, and a police officer descends the stairs with a gun in hand.

"John, you are going to prison if you don't tell me where you hid those girls you murdered."

"I told you I didn't murder anyone."

The policeman puts the gun to Mark's head, and Mark begins to whimper.

"Look, mister. I told you I am not John, and I need to get home to my wife. She is waiting for me. What are you doing? Please don't shoot me. I am innocent!"

"The sentence for you is death. The execution will take place at six tonight. What would you like for your last meal? Will it be pizza or a hamburger?"

"I should have anything I want," says Mark.

"What will it be? Pizza or a hamburger?"

"I told you, you bastard! I haven't decided."

"Good! Pizza it is."

"What did the District Attorney say? Can I hope for a stay of execution?" asks Mark.

"It is possible, but you only have an hour. I will call the District Attorney for you."

"Barbara, would you call Mark for me? Maybe he will answer if you call," says Samantha.

"Sure hold on. I will dial now."

"Barbara, I haven't given you his cellphone number."

7

———

Mark is distraught; he is sure he will never see Samantha again. He needs to get free before execution.

"John! Look at me."

"Who are you, and why are you dressed in a prison outfit?" asks Mark.

"You know you are here in prison, and I am your cellmate. When are you getting the needle, huh?"

"I am waiting for the District Attorney to get me a stay of execution."

"Who told you that shit?"

"That cop who visited me a few minutes ago."

"Don't listen to that 'prick'. That guy isn't a cop. He is a guard here at this prison. He tells all new inmates they can get a stay of execution."

"I got to get out of here. Can you untie my hands?"

"You ain't ever getting out of here alive."

"Please, mister. I got to get out of here! I am pleading… Hey, where are you going? Please don't leave me."

"You are a lost soul, John. See you around."

"My name is not John!" says Mark.

As soon as the prisoner leaves the basement, a woman starts descending the basement stairs.

"Johnny baby, it is mamma. I am here to see you. You know how much I love you, Johnny."

Mark decides to start playing into this. Six PM is less than an hour away.

"Mamma, please get me out of here. Mamma, I am innocent. I do not know why I am here."

"Johnny, I love you so much. I remember when you were such a small boy. You were such a good boy."

"Mamma, please come over and hug me. Please run your hands through my hair like you used to do."

"I can't, Johnny. There is a glass barrier between us. I am just visiting you."

"No, mamma, there is no barrier. Please come over here. I want to hug you, mamma."

"Oh, Johnny, my favorite little boy, just place your head on my shoulder. That's a good boy."

"Mamma, you know I am a good little boy. Please get me out of here. Please untie my hands."

"Johnny, you know I cannot do that. They won't let me."

"Mamma, please?"

"Here, my little boy, take this nail file. You will want to keep your fingernails clean for when I come back to visit you."

"Mamma, please don't leave me," says Mark.

"I will be back, Johnny. I love you."

———

"Julia, I just received a call about the missing husband. The wife is worried that something happened to him. She says that his car is still at the grocery store, and the store clerk remembers him being there," says Bobbie.

"Bobbie, we have something even bigger to check on. A chief over in Cleveland had called me a half-hour ago describing a scene over at an old school. There appears to be a homicide. He didn't give me many details, but is looking for our assistance," says Julia.

"I will give Richard a call and ask him to watch our little darlings for a while," says Bobbie.

"OK Bobbie. Amanda, we will need you to come with us. We will do DNA testing as required," says Julia.

———

Mark immediately starts to maneuver the nail file for cutting the ropes holding his hands to the desk. He knows he must work fast before someone else comes down to visit him.

There is loud music heard on the floor immediately above Mark. He starts to ascend the basement stairs after he frees his hands and then his feet. Opening the basement door at the top of the stairs, Mark slowly walks past the room where a guy is sitting listening to the loud music and watching porn on the television. Just as Mark is placing his hand on the door leading to his freedom, he feels a heavy blow to the back of his head and then blacks out hitting the floor.

"Nice to see you are finally awake, John."

"Who the hell are you, and why am I tied to this desk?" asks Mark.

"I am the Warden of this prison, and I am sorry to inform you there will not be a stay of execution for you. I just finished talking to the District Attorney."

"I must beg of you. I am not guilty. I am not the guy you think I am. Please let me go. I don't want to die!"

"Well, we haven't talked about your failed escape. I don't take too kindly to inmates who try to escape my prison. So, this is what I am going to do."

"What are you going to do with those…?"

"Give me your hand! Now hold still."

"No, no, please, not my left hand! Ah…owe, owe…you bastard!"

"That wasn't so bad, was it? Let's see another finger.."

"Oh, no…," cries Mark as another one of his fingers is cut off.

"No, no, not my fingers! I am a guitar player, please….owe…owe.."

"All done! I guess your career playing the guitar has suddenly ended."

Mark writhes with pain and sees three of his fingers severed at the first joint. Before the Warden ascends the basement stairway, he wraps Mark's hand in a dirty rag.

"Barbara, how did you know Mark's cellphone number?"

"Samantha don't you remember? You gave me his number."

"I don't remember that," says Samantha.

Anyway, he isn't answering my call either," says Barbara.

"Barbara, what are you doing?"

"What is the matter with you, Samantha?"

"You know what I am talking about, Barbara."

"Samantha, I think you are tired and too upset. Please stay here with me tonight, and we will start again in the morning."

"Hello, my name is Doctor Stewart. I hear you have an injury. Let me see. Oh, my, we need to sew those wounds to stop the bleeding."

"Doctor, my fingers are down there on the floor. If you work quickly, you can get me to the hospital so they can sew them back on."

"That won't be necessary. Hold on while I sew these up. You won't feel anything."

Mark cries each time the doctor pushes the sewing needle into the ends of his finger stumps, threading stitches.

"You have to take me to the hospital," says Mark.

"You will be all right. I will come and dress those wounds tomorrow."

"Tomorrow! I won't be here tomorrow. My execution is in fifteen minutes," says Mark.

"I will see you tomorrow. Now be sure to keep those wounds clean."

"You bastard! Get back here! Where the hell are you going?" asks Mark.

"Hello, my name is Chief Julia Lillus, and this is my Deputy Bobbie Peltz and my Forensics Specialist, Amanda Alexandria. We represent the Harford Police Department."

"Hi, I am Chief of Police for the community of Cleveland."

"Fill us in what you have here," says Julia.

"Down there. You won't like what you see! Don't say I didn't warn you."

Barbara lies sleeping on the couch while Samantha can't sleep. Samantha reaches over to Barbara's cellphone and pushes the button to view recent calls and texts. To her astonishment, she notices Barbara has many conversations sent and received from her husband, Mark.

"Barbara Jones, wake up!"

"Wha…what? Samantha, what is it? Did you have a bad dream?"

"You slut! My best friend and screwing my husband?"

"Samantha, what are you saying? You need to get some sleep."

"I have seen all the calls and texts you have made to Mark and the calls he has made to you. You are a fucking slut!"

"Barbara, please! I am choking! Let me go! I…I…can't breathe… You …..are going to….to…to… pay for fucking my husband. Now… now, where is…is he?" asks Samantha struggling to breathe.

"Die, you bitch," hollers Barbara as she presses both her thumbs onto Samantha's windpipe until she no longer hears Samantha breathing.

"No, no! Please. Who are you? Why can't I see your face?" screams Mark.

"I am your Executioner! In five minutes, you will die."

"No, no, you mustn't. I am not guilty. Let me go!"

Mark is sweating, and tears are rolling down his cheeks as he watches the second hand of the clock make its round to twelve signifying six o'clock.

The Executioner walks over to a table. Mark notices a tank of oxygen and a tank of acetylene as the torch is lit.

"What are you going to do, screams Mark! No, no, please don't…."

"Oh my God, Julia! What happened down here?" asks Bobbie as she starts to cover her eyes.

"Amanda, do you think you can get DNA samples?"

"I will try. The burns…they are pretty bad. I still do not see the body's head."

"Over there, on the table," says Julia pointing to the table in the corner.

"Whoever did this, burned his neck right through until it fell off of the body. This poor soul has had fingers cut off as well," says Bobbie.

THE DEED IS DONE

There is a knock on the door to Barbara's home.

"Hello, sis."

"Hello, Johnny. Come in. How is your drama studies coming? Is it working out for you at that old high school with all of your costumes and props?"

"Yup, no problems at all. Everything is just fine."

"Were you careful not to leave any clues behind?"

"Everything is fine. The authorities will never suspect the neighborhood butcher. After all, I honestly don't know who killed your lover, Mark. Many people could have done it. He was convicted, and the sentence was death, and carried out."

"Yes, Johnny, I agree. Many people could have killed him."

"Sis, where is Samantha? Has she been convicted yet?"

"Yes, and she was sentenced to death for her crime, and it was carried out."

"What did you do to her?"

"Johnny, never mind! I have taken care of it. No one will find the body."

"What do you have for us, Chief?" asks Julia.

"It is hard to say, Ms. Julia. No one uses this old high school building. Down the hall on the second floor, there is a room with all sorts of costumes and props."

"Yeah, probably the room was for the drama class supplies," says Julia.

"It does appear the poor soul down there suffered immensely. Fingers on the left hand have been severed at the first joint. He has been beaten all over his body and his head, well what is visible anyway... It appears his head was removed from his body by the use of an acetylene torch, says the Chief."

"We have a missing person case, and the wife is from this area. There could be a connection. Maybe this body is her husband," says Julia.

"Well, where do we start?" asks the Chief of Police in Cleveland.

"Amanda is collecting DNA samples from the body, and we will need to go around this building to see if our murderer is using this school as a hideout and an execution site. Hopefully, there will be something we can get more DNA samples from, like a room or area where he/she might have eaten," says Julia.

"So, sis, what are we going to do now that your lover Mark and that bitch Samantha is executed?" asks Johnny.

"We will need to move on. We can no longer stay here. The authorities might think that we were the ones who executed those two," says Barbara.

"What about the call to the police? They can trace her cellphone number, and it will show it to be here at our home."

"Not a chance, Johnny, it is why I took that phone across two counties from here."

"I don't know why you had to do that instead of just breaking the phone," says Johnny.

"I had to. I didn't want it to look obvious that I knew Samantha and was fucking her husband, and besides, it will show the last place she was is where I put the phone."

"Where will we go?" asks Johnny.

"We are going to skip out of this city, and we are going tonight. I am sorry, Johnny, that you won't be able to collect your drama class costumes. I know how much you like them."

"I will have to find another school and work my way into it. Maybe I should pose as a janitor in a school that is alive with students. The game of charades is rather fun. I don't think I need a reason for acting or executing," says Johnny.

"Get all of the practice you can because I will need an Executioner for my next cheating subject."

"Are you ever going to get married, Barbara?"

"Hell no! Maybe if I like him fucking me, maybe. Besides, I need the variety. Not all male cocks are the same, you know...."

After the three ladies from the Harford Police Department have finished with their investigation at the old abandoned high school, they make their way back to the office.

"What do you make of this, Julia?" asks Bobbie.

"I don't know, but I would like you and Richard to go to the address where the missing persons call originated," says Julia.

"Julia, I was able to get some samples from a supposed break room. I will run them against the body samples to find a match," says Amanda.

"OK, we won't need a Coroner's report. It is quite evident what the cause of death was, but we need a motive and who is the body," says Julia.

"I am going back over tomorrow to see if I can find out who is using that high school and for what purpose," says Bobbie.

Bobbie and Richard arrive at the address where the missing persons call originated only to find the house vacant. The nearby neighbors are questioned, but no one knew the people living there or when/where they went.

Bobbie drops Richard off at their home to relieve the nanny from watching their children. She goes on over to Cleveland.

In passing by the old high school, she notices an old truck parked in the front of the building.

"Hello, is anyone here?" asks Bobbie as she opens the entrance door.

"Yes, I am the caretaker for this old building. You must be with the police?"

"Yes, my name is Deputy Bobbie Peltz."

"I am so glad you are here. I cannot get to the basement or the drama room on the second floor. I keep this place clean, you see, even though there isn't anyone here."

"No one here? The room up there has all sorts of costumes in it, and it appears someone has been living there by the looks of the food scraps left on the table," says Bobbie.

"Well, there is a guy who stays here. He practices his drama studies and goes by the name of John. But I do not know anymore about him. He seems friendly enough," says the caretaker.

"You don't know his last name? How about where he lives?" asks Bobbie.

"I know nothing more than I told you, and I believe he lives up there in the drama room. By the way, what is going on around here? Why the police barrier tape?" asks the caretaker.

"There have been some unfortunate events here. You will have to wait to clean those areas until the investigation is complete," answers Bobbie.

———

"Johnny, all the time we have been together, and you have never made any advances toward me. What is up with that?" asks Barbara.

"What do you mean, Barbara?"

"Come on, Johnny! You know, fucking me?"

"Barbara, I am not that type of a guy. You know that! I don't ever touch women, let alone my own sister."

As Barbara moves closer to Johnny, she takes his hand and places it on her breast.

"Johnny, do you feel that? Feel those bumps? They are my nipples. Squeeze them."

"Barbara, please don't ask me to do that...I..I..."

"Johnny put your hand down here. Put your finger in the crevice of my pants and move it up and down."

"No, Barbara, please don't ask me to do that?"

"OK, OK, Johnny. It has been a long trip getting here, so why don't you just lay down here on the bed and take a nap."

"What are we going to do next, Barbara?"

"Just relax, Johnny. We will talk about it later."

As Johnny settles down on the bed and closes his eyes to relax, Barbara continues her prowess of satiating her sexual needs.

"Johnny, just relax while I massage your shoulders. Raise your arms. Yeah, that's it."

"Barbara, that feels good. You do great massages."

"Just relax, Johnny. Raise your arms straight up like you are doing a stretch. Yeah, that's it, now breathe deeply and forget about all of your troubles."

"Barbara, why are you massaging my arms?"

"Johnny, there is great tension in them, I feel it. Now relax while I massage your palms. There are many sensory nerves in your palms, and massaging them releases stress throughout your entire body."

"Barbara, what are you doing with my legs?"

"Relax, Johnny. I am going to massage your legs as well. They are just like your arms. Very sensory nerves are there as well."

As Barbara finishes the massage, she starts to slip her clothes off and stands naked at Johnny's head.

"Johnny, you can open your eyes now. Do you feel very relaxed now?"

"Barbara, why are your clothes off? I don't want to see you like that!"

"Come on, Johnny. Haven't you ever seen a naked female before?"

"No, I don't want to. I will keep my eyes closed."

"Suit yourself, Johnny, I will just take upon myself to self-serve."

"Hey, why are my hands and feet tied to the bedposts? Barbara, release me...what are you doing?"

"Settle down Johnny. Now just relax."

"Barbara, stop! Stop touching me down there! What are you doing?"

"Johnny, haven't you had a 'hard-on' before?"

"What?"

"For heaven's sake, Johnny. Haven't you ever experienced your cock being stiff?"

"Yes, I try to hide it. I don't like it to do that."

"Well, I need it that way. So just relax and feel me as I settle down on you."

"Barbara, what are you doing?"

"Sit still while I lower my pussy on your cock! Do you feel that, Johnny? Doesn't it feel good?"

"Barbara, I don't want to do this. Please stop! Oh, oh, I feel something moving. Barbara, I need to pee."

"Relax, Johnny, you will be all right."

"Barbara, I am going to pee….oh, oh…..awe…"

Just as Johnny 'cums', Barbara places her finger on her clit and massages it until she, too, 'cums'.

"Barbara, I am furious at you! You made me hard, and I never want that, and you made me pee all over you or something."

"Johnny, you poor idiot. You just experienced sex and what it feels like to have it with a female. Now go take a shower and wash off your cock."

———

Julia, I just spoke to the caretaker over there at the high school, and he said a guy named John stays there to practice his drama studies. He says he knows nothing more. This is a strange case," says Bobbie.

Bobbie, see if you can find any clues, at the high school, to the whereabouts of this John. I am pretty sure he will return if he is not guilty of anything," says Julia.

———

"Barbara, why did you do that to me?"

"Johnny, you know I have an appetite for sex. It is the main reason we are doing this. The only problem is that I get tired of screwing the same gentlemen, and, well, you know the rest."

"But Barbara, I am your brother! You had sex with your brother!"

"You may be my brother, but a cock is a cock, and that is all I need."

"Barbara, you can't do that to me ever again."

"Johnny, I won't have to if I can find a guy real soon! Now, this is the plan. I will solicit myself to some guys here, in town. I am sure at least one of them will take me up on it. Meanwhile, you need to find a suitable place to set up your drama room. By the way, can't you just strangle the guy or something? Do you need to go through all of that drama?"

"Barbara, I am an accomplished drama artist. I have to continue to practice my intrigue. You do know I will head an actual play soon for all to see, and none of it will be fake or staged."

"All right, Johnny, I have heard that many times. Don't you think you are taking this way to far?"

"Be careful, Barbara. You know that crossing me sets my multiple personalities off. I don't know what I might do to you should that happen."

"Johnny, maybe you can get stuck in the personality of a sex lord, and we can just screw as much as we want."

"Barbara, I told you I do not ever want that to happen again! I will not tolerate it!"

"Julia, did Amanda get over to the address where the phone call originated and take DNA samples?" asks Bobbie.

"Yes, and she is now comparing the sample lifted from the doorknob to the sample taken from the rim of the cup found in the drama room at the high school," answers Julia.

"I am curious whether there is a match leading us to some connectivity in this case," says Bobbie.

DECEPTION LEADS TO DEATH

"Hey, you, young man! How about you and I go get some drinks," says Barbara.

"Well, I don't know. I am just leaving work and on my way home to my wife."

"Oh, come on. No harm here, I just want to talk. I am new to this town, and I would like to get to know people here. Look, just one drink and some small talk, and then you can be on your way. I want you to tell me a little bit about this town of yours," says Barbara.

"I guess I can do that."

"Tell me about yourself. You say you are married, and do you have any kids?" asks Barbara.

"Yes, I am married, and I have a boy and a girl."

The conversation between Barbara and this guy continues for about a half-hour before he decides it is time to leave the bar.

"Barbara, if you don't mind, I need to get back to my home. My wife will be worried about me."

"Sure, Lewis, is it? I mean, your name?"

"Yes, Barbara, my name is Lewis."

"Let me walk out with you. I need to get back to my home as well," says Barbara.

"Oh, I am sorry Lewis, I dropped my purse."

Just as Barbara bends to reach down to pick up her purse, Lewis also bends down to pick it up for her. Barbara swiftly crosses one of her legs over Lewis's arm, and as he straightens up, his head gets stuck on her skirt, and it rises with his head showing Barbara's panties.

"Oh, I am so sorry, Barbara. It was an accident. I didn't realize my head was in a position to lift your skirt."

"You purposely reached around my leg to get my purse. What did you think would happen? You are a pervert! You wanted to see what was under my skirt!"

"No, I did not!"

"Police! Police! This man is trying to rape me!" exclaims Barbara.

"Settle down, miss. Tell me what happened," says the police officer.

"I dropped my purse, and he bent down, crossing my leg to pick it up and upon rising lifted my skirt high enough to show my panties. It is good I have panties on, or he would have seen my pussy. That is what he was hoping for, I am sure."

"Barbara, you are wrong! It was an accident. I am a married man! I would do anything like that on purpose! It was an accident!" exclaims Lewis.

"Bobbie, Amanda has concluded her tests, and yes, there is connectivity. The DNA taken from the cup at the high school matches the DNA found on the doorknob of the address where the phone call came from," says Julia.

"This is interesting. Why did someone at the high school go to that address and make a missing person call? Could the lady making the call claiming her husband was missing be the person who did the torture in the basement, and if so, why?" asks Bobbie.

"Bobbie, I think there was possibly a third person involved in this case, and it isn't the caretaker. He was out of town, and Richard verified that," says Julia.

"Julia, I am going back over to the address and search for more clues to maybe uncover a third person," says Bobbie.

"Good, Bobbie. I will be able to join you when I get this paperwork out of the way."

"Listen mister, Lewis is it?"

"Yes, my name is Lewis."

"I am going to take you to my Department for further questioning and hold you until this matter is resolved."

"Officer, I did nothing wrong. I was not trying to rape her!"

"Come on! Just around the corner is the Police Department," says the police officer.

Just as Lewis and the police officer round the corner, Lewis is pushed against the wall by the officer.

"Johnny, get him on the ground and hold him down," yells Barbara.

"What the hell are you doing? You aren't a police officer! Barbara, what is the meaning of this?" asks Lewis.

"Shut up, Lewis! I am going to ride your cock as it has never been ridden before!" exclaims Barbara.

"Who and what the hell are you, Barbara? Officer, this woman is going to rape me!"

"That's right, Lewis, and you better enjoy it because it will be the last fuck you will ever have!" exclaims Johnny.

Barbara continues with her typical ritual. She pulls Lewis's pants off and pulls his cock out of his underwear and proceeds to stroke it until it gets hard. She then pulls off her panties and lowers herself onto Lewis stroking his cock, now, moving up and down inside her.

"Barbara, I can't watch this," says Johnny.

"Just keep pinning his hands down and make sure the gag stays into his mouth."

Lewis is in agony as Barbara strokes his cock with her pussy. He thinks of his wife and kids. He doesn't want to 'cum' in Barbara, but he cannot stop it as he blasts his load into her.

"Now then Lewis, see it wasn't so bad. You got off with someone other than your wife. I bet my fuck was better than any you had with your wife! Johnny, I am done with him. Do with him what you want, but make it fast," says Barbara.

"This man has been involved with rape. I can see his 'cum' running down your leg as you stand there and your panties in his hand. The pig! The police officer has brought him into court, and he is found guilty. I am the Executioner, and justice must be served," says Johnny.

"What is the sentence Executioner?" asks Barbara.

"The sentence is a beheading. Help me drag Lewis to the dumpster and place his neck at the rim of the opening. I don't want blood all over the street," says Johnny.

"Julia!"

"Yes, Betsy, what is it?"

"I just received a call that another missing persons, a husband, has been posted over in Stanton County. I wonder if there is a connection," says Betsy.

"I don't know Betsy. Get a hold of the Police Department over there," says Julia.

"Barbara, help me close the dumpster cover!"

"Executioner, I don't believe the sentence can be carried out in this fashion," says Barbara.

"Yes, it can. We just keep slamming the cover until Lewis's head is severed from his neck."

Just as Lewis feels the excruciating pain with the first closure of the dumpster lid, he thinks of his wife and kids and cries. The second blow pushes Lewis unconscious, and the fourth blow severs his head.

"Executioner, is the sentence complete?" asks Barbara.

"Yes, the sentence is complete."

"Johnny, what do we do now?"

"Well, the Executioner has done his job, so I guess it is up to the Sanitation Engineer to clean up this mess."

"Ma'am, do you know this guy who seems to have lost his head?" asks the Sanitation Engineer.

"No, my brother Johnny and I just found him like that," says Barbara.

"OK, I will just put the rest of his body in the dumpster and clean up this blood on the pavement. It will only take a minute."

"Well, Johnny, the Sanitation Engineer cleaned up the mess," says Barbara.

"Yes, he did a good job. The poor devil who lost his head. I wonder how it happened……," says Johnny.

"Hello, yes, this is Chief Julia Lillus. How can I help you?"

"Yes, my name is Commissioner Joseph, and we, over here in Stanton County, have our first missing persons, and we need help."

"OK, how can we help?"

"We would like your assistance in figuring out this missing person report. We heard you are working, currently, on a missing person case, and your Department holds a high status among the communities," says Commissioner Joseph.

"Well, thank you for the compliments. How about we work this case and keep you abreast of the outcome? I have a feeling your case, being a missing husband, and our current case, a missing husband, might have things in common," says Julia.

"That would be great, Miss Julia. We are unsure of how to handle this case."

"Please call me Julia. You need to know I am not the formal type of person."

"Johnny, you must know a missing persons reporting will be made by Lewis's wife soon," says Barbara.

"Yeah, I know, but there is no way they can pin us to it. There was no one around when the Executioner did his deed. Did anyone see you with that guy at the bar?"

"No, Johnny, we were the only ones in the bar, and I don't think the guy at the counter made us out. It was pretty dark in there, as bars go," says Barbara.

"Barbara, we will have to lay low for a while, and you will need to find a guy who is not attached to anyone."

"Johnny, there is no way I can figure that out when trying to lure a guy. Besides, if I get desperate, I will…"

"No way, Barbara. You are not going to fuck me ever again! Can't you just satisfy yourself?"

"No, I need a cock in my pussy to satisfy my indulgence."

"Maybe I get a…what do you call them things you girls use?"

"Johnny, you are referring to a dildo. You are so shallow, Johnny. I need a real cock when fucking because the release of 'cum' is what turns me on. A dildo won't do it for me."

"Well, Barbara, you are just going to have to suffer a bit, I guess."

"Hmm, maybe Johnny, maybe not."

"Richard, will you please go over to Stanton County and interview the woman who called in her missing husband?" asks Julia.

"Yes, ma'am, I am on my way."

"Who is watching the kiddos, Richard?" asks Julia.

"Oh, Bobbie is, unless you need her for something."

"No, I am good with that Richard. 'Anything to keep you away from her'."

"What did you say, Julia?"

"Oh, nothing. I was just saying how much I love your kiddos."

"Mrs. Balster? I am Officer Richard Peltz. May I come in?"

"Oh, yes. Have you heard anything about my missing husband?"

"No, not yet, Mrs. Balster."

"Please call me Vicki."

"OK, Vicki. Tell me about the time when you discovered your husband was missing."

"Lewis, my husband was at work a couple of days ago when he called me and told me he would be a little late because of his work. I delayed dinner for him that evening. I expected him to be home at around six o'clock. When seven o'clock came around, I got worried. I called his cell, but I just got his answering message."

"Vicki, I hate to ask you this, but do you think your husband, Lewis, was maybe seeing another woman? We have to ask this."

"Officer Peltz, my Lewis is a very dedicated husband, and we have two young children he loves very dearly. We have a very close relationship in our marriage, and we think the world of each other."

"Here, Vicki. Please take this tissue. I am sorry to have asked that, but we must get all the facts to help us in finding your husband. Have you tried calling him recently?"

"Yes, I have called him every hour on the hour, but no answer."

"Vicky, is there anything else you might tell me that might help us locate Lewis, your husband?"

"No, I can't think of anything. All I can think of is the dinners we have had at Banjos. Those dinners were special."

"Banjos? What is Banjos?" asks Richard.

"Banjos is a diner/bar just down on the main street. Lewis and I celebrated our latest wedding anniversary there. It is such a special place."

"Thank you, Vicki, for your time. If there is anything else, please call me. Here is my card. We will be in touch with you on anything we uncover," says Richard.

"Thank you, Officer Peltz."

BARBARA AND JOHNNY

"Johnny, I am getting sick of the theatrical antics you act out," says Barbara.

"What do you mean, Barbara?"

"Why can't you just get rid of the bodies like you, Johnny, and not some cooked up personality that makes you into someone else."

"I told you, Barbara, you shouldn't cross me about those things."

"Why not, Johnny? I am a horny nymphomaniac and wish I had the freedom to fuck any guy I come into contact with."

"Well, you are fucking every guy you come in contact with."

"Yeah, but your changeable personalities hamper my true feelings of satisfaction. You are pathetic, Johnny!"

"Barbara, I am warning you!"

"Where are you going, you 'ill-human'?" asks Barbara.

Johnny leaves the room and goes into his bedroom.

"Who are you?" asks Barbara as Johnny emerges from his bedroom.

"My name is the great Casanova, and I am here to eradicate your sins!"

"Eradicate my sins? What the hell are you talking about, Johnny?"

"Who is Johnny? I am the great Casanova. Now, what sins do you have to eradicate?"

"Last I knew, Casanova does not eradicate sins. As a matter of fact, he functions in sin," says Barbara.

"Well, I understand you have a love for sex? Am I correct in this?" asks Casanova.

"Oh, you are starting to see it my way, Johnny."

"Who the hell is Johnny?"

"Casanova, just get on the bed and eradicate my sin!"

"Julia, the woman whose husband is missing, Vicki, gave me a clue that may help us in the case. She mentioned that she and her husband, Lewis, would go to a diner/bar called Banjos. I went and visited Banjos and asked the bartender if he had seen Lewis recently. He told me that a couple of nights ago, Lewis came into his establishment with a woman. The bartender said that the appearance of those two did not give him the feeling the guy was happy to be there with her. He kept looking at his watch, but the woman kept him in the conversation for about a half-hour. He said they left together. Vicki did not believe that Lewis was seeing another woman," says Richard.

"Do you feel that this Vicki knows her husband enough to make that statement?" asks Julia.

"Well, they have two young children that she says loves their daddy dearly as he does love them, also very dearly. Vicki is a nice young attractive woman, so I cannot believe Lewis could do better."

"I know Richard, but stranger things have happened with these type cases. I do have a hunch Vicki and Lewis are in love and that Lewis would not go out on her with another woman. Why don't you go back to Banjos and see if you can get a clue to where those two went after leaving the establishment," says Julia.

"Hey Casanova, you sure know how to eradicate sins! My entire ass is quivering from that fuck," says Barbara.

"Who the hell is Casanova, Barbara? Look at you! Did you take my advice and 'do yourself'? How did you manage to get 'cum' on your leg?"

"Don't worry, Johnny. There are things a woman can do to make it look real."

"Man, I smell like a wet pussy!"

"Oh, Johnny, how do you know what a wet pussy smells like?"

"Barbara, you aren't a rose, you know. I can smell your fucks every time. Anyhow, I feel down there like I did when you raped me, Barbara."

"Johnny, haven't you ever experienced a 'wet dream' before?"

"Julia, a guy who was across the street from Banjos that night, saw a man and lady walking out of the establishment. He said it looked like she dropped her purse, and the guy bent down to pick it up for her, and when he stood back up, his head lifted her skirt high enough to see her pink panties. Some kind of commotion came about, and a police officer arrived on the scene as the woman was screaming," says Richard.

"Did the guy see what happened after that?" asks Julia.

"Well, he said that all he could see was the police officer took the man around the corner. He said it looked like the officer dragged him, and the woman followed shortly after. They were then out of view, and it sounded like someone was emptying their trash in the dumpster," says Richard.

"OK, thanks Richard. I will follow up with you in a little bit. I have to make a phone call," says Julia.

"Commissioner Joseph? This is Julia from the Harford Police Department."

"Yes, Julia, what is it?"

"Did you encounter an officer detaining a man with possibly a woman? It could have been for an assault or something, around the establishment called Banjos?"

"No, Julia. When would this have happened?"

"A couple of nights ago."

"No, Julia. We haven't had any officers dispatched in that area for at least three weeks."

"OK, thanks Commissioner Joseph. I will get back to you as soon as we check out a few things," says Julia.

"Johnny, it has been a couple of days, and I am getting in 'heat' again," says Barbara.

"What do you mean by getting in 'heat'?"

"Johnny, you are so dense! I mean, I need to be fucked! My pussy yearns for a cock! Do you get it, Johnny?"

"Barbara, why do you need to be fucked so much?"

"I am a nymphomaniac, and that means I yearn to be fucked as much as you would have an appetite for eating food."

"How did that happen, Barbara?"

"I don't know. It is probably from birth, just like your multiple personalities."

"I don't have multiple personalities, Barbara."

"Yes, you do, and I need to be fucked real soon!"

"Don't look at me, Barbara. I never want that ever again, especially from my sister."

"Come on, Johnny. It won't hurt you. Either you or I need to get another man."

"We can't take the chance yet, Barbara!"

"Richard, I want you to go over to Vicki's home and have her call her husband's cell phone when I call you. Bobbie and I are going over to Banjos. I think I am piecing together something," says Julia.

"Richard, you know what it means when Julia has a hunch. We are about to solve a crime," says Bobbie.

"Come on, Bobbie, let's get going and Richard, wait for my call," says Julia.

Outside the establishment Banjos, Julia and Bobbie pull up to the curb.

"Bobbie let's stand here for a minute while I call Richard to have Vicki make the call to her husband," says Julia.

"Richard? Did you explain to Vicki what she was to do?"

"Yes, Julia. She is dialing now," says Richard.

"Bobbie, do you hear that?"

"Yeah, I hear a phone ringing. Where is it coming from?"

"Over here, Bobbie, around the corner from Banjos."

"It sounds like it…"

"Yes, Bobbie, it sounds like it is coming from the dumpster, here," says Julia.

"Oh, Julia, it smells real bad over here."

"It smells like a dead body. Help me lift the lid," says Julia.

"Holy hell, there is the ringing cell phone and a body decapitated. It has to be Vicki's husband," says Bobbie.

"Richard, please thank Vicki and tell her we will get back to her," says Julia.

"Bobbie let's get the Coroner down here," says Julia.

Back at the office, Richard, Bobbie, and Julia try to piece together what they have found out.

———

"OK, we have two murders we have been trying to solve, and each of the murders was committed unusually and bizarrely. One murder is a missing persons, a husband. The other murder is a missing persons that appears to be the same as the other, a missing husband. It is kind of a weird clue, but the Coroner said the latest murder, possibly Lewis, showed signs of having intercourse fairly recently," says Julia.

"Do you suppose Lewis, if that is who the body is, was seeing another woman, Julia?" asks Bobbie.

"It appears that may be the case, Bobbie."

"Well, I do not buy that. I believe Vicki when she said she was sure Lewis was not seeing another woman," says Richard.

"Then who did Lewis, or this guy, have sex with that night? It certainly was not Vicki," says Bobbie.

"Let's not dwell on the sex situation right now. I do not see a connection with the two murders at this time. Richard, call Vicki and have her go to the Coroners' to identify if the body is her husband Lewis. Then, I want you to frequent Banjos for a couple of nights in plain clothes. Be observant of who comes and goes and especially a woman who might come in with a guy. Call me if you suspect anything unusual," says Julia.

"Richard, please be careful and no dining with women," says Bobbie.

"Don't worry, Bobbie. Julia, can Bobbie and I take the rest of the afternoon off before I have to leave for Banjos?" asks Richard.

"Sure. Do you need a baby-sitter for the occasion?" asks Julia.

"That would be perfect if you would, Julia," says Richard.

"Richard, what do you have in mind for this afternoon away from the kids?" asks Bobbie.

"I made a reservation at the Silent Sleeper Motel."

"Richard, you rascal!" exclaims Bobbie.

"Oh, boy, not another little Peltz…hmmm," whispers Julia.

———

"Johnny, whether you like it or not, I am going out tonight and get me some cock."

"Barbara, you had better not!"

"Either that, or you will give it to me!"

"No way!"

"I am going to bring him here, so you don't need to follow me," says Barbara.

BANJOS

Later that day, at Banjos.

"Richard, how are things? Are you in place yet?" asks Julia.

"I am right here in Banjos and it is quite the place. Very quiet," says Richard.

"Julia, I will be leaving my tracker on so you can see where I go if I need to leave here."

"Good idea Richard."

"Hey mister, would you like some company?"

"Sure, take a seat," says Richard.

"My name is Barbara. I am new here, and I would love to know more about this area."

"Would you like a drink, Barbara?"

"Yes, sure…..Make it a Scotch on the Rocks."

"So, Barbara, where are you from?"

"Oh, I am from a small town in Ohio. Have you lived here your entire time?"

"No, Barbara, but I have lived in this town for quite a few years. It feels like I have been here since I was born."

"Mister, are you married?"

"My name is Richard, and yes, I am married, and I have three children, all little girls."

"Wow, you have been busy, I mean you are so lucky to have children."

"Barbara, do you have any children? Married?"

"No, neither. I haven't been able to find the right man to settle down with."

"I am sure the right guy will show up. It sometimes takes time."

"Do you have pictures of your wife and kids?"

"I sure do. Take a look."

"Wow, your wife is beautiful and so young. No offense, but I see where your girls' look's come from."

"None took. My wife is a beauty and my whole world, and I am proud that she gave me my children."

"Oh, how time flies. I must be getting back."

"I don't see your car Barbara, and it is raining outside. Do you live far from here?"

"Oh, just across town a bit. I walked here, not realizing it might rain."

"Come on, I will drive you home," says Richard.

"This is it, Richard. Would you please come in for some tea before you venture back to your wife and children?"

THE SEDUCTION

"Bobbie, this is Julia. Is your nanny still at your home?"

"Yes, she is staying the night because of the rain," answers Bobbie.

"Good, I need you down here. Richard has moved from Banjos across town, it appears, and I do not know why. We need to find him and make sure he isn't in danger," says Julia.

"I will be right there, Julia."

"Richard, here is your tea. I will join you in a moment. I need to freshen up a bit," says Barbara.

Richard quickly dials Julia from his cell phone, but before he can talk to her, Barbara enters the room.

"Barbara, what is going on? I don't think you are reading me correctly," says Richard.

"Richard, come on, have you not ever seen your wife dressed like this? With three children, I am sure she looked exactly like this or even less than the clothes I have on. Do you like what you see? Can you see my big erect nipples under this transparent top, and oh, how about my pussy? See my pink lips? I shaved just for you."

"Look, Barbara, you have the wrong idea. I am not looking for sex."

"You may not be Richard, but I am! You see, I am what you call a nymphomaniac. Do you know what that means, Richard? It means I need a man; I need a cock between my legs as much as I need to eat. Now, get out of your clothes and let's get to it!"

"Barbara, this isn't going to happen. You need professional help."

"Johnny, come here, please," says Barbara.

"Ma'am, I do not know Johnny. My name is Judge Masters, and I am here to give the sentence."

"What sentence?" asks Richard.

"You have raped this woman!"

"Johnny, no, no, this is my man. Let me get fucked. You know I need it!"

"Bobbie, what is the number of the home Richard is at?"

"The tracker says 100 South Jefferson St., Julia."

"We are on South Jefferson now…oh, here is 100. Quick Bobbie, you go to the back door, and I will go to the front," says Julia.

"Barbara, you don't need to do this!"

"Lay down Richard and unzip those pants," says Barbara.

"You are sentenced," says Judge Masters.

"Johnny, get away from him!"

"You are sentenced, you slut. You have been raping men, and your sentence is death!"

"Johnny, have you gone crazy? It is me, your sister, Barbara."

"I am the Executioner, and you will die!"

"No, Johnny!" exclaims Richard.

"The slut will die!"

As soon as Johnny, the Executioner, issues his command, he slices Barbara's throat with a knife.

"Freeze, mister!" exclaims Julia.

"Richard, are you OK?" asks Bobbie.

"Yes, I am. I am so happy to see you. Please help me get this woman off of me," says Richard.

"Geesh, Richard. Were you watching her parade around like that? She might as well not have any clothes. Did she…ah…did she…?

"No, Bobbie, she didn't get to me, but if you hadn't arrived when you did, well, who knows what would have happened."

"Richard, I know what would have happened. Her snatch would have taken you prisoner!"

"Oh, Bobbie, let's not think about that! By the way, I did not revel in her clothes or lack thereof."

"OK, mister, who the hell are you? Hold your hands behind your back," yells Julia.

"I am Judge Masters and the Executioner. I have to carry out the sentence. She raped them, and she killed them. She was a slut and had to be stopped. She fucked that guy in Cleveland, but the Executioner had to kill him for raping her. I am the Executioner," mumbles Johnny.

"Bobbie, you go ahead and help Richard. I will get this guy to the car," says Julia.

THE CASES ARE EXPLAINED

After Julia stops at Commissioner Joseph's house and explains the conclusion to the missing person in Stanton County, she then travels to the village of Cleveland and gives the report to the authorities and releases Johnny to them.

Bobbie takes Richard back to their home while she continues to Vicki's house to see if her husband Lewis, was the guy murdered in the dumpster.

It has been a long night, and the Harford Police Department staff agreed to reconvene in the morning.

"Did Richard and you get a good night's rest, Bobbie? How about you, Amanda?" asks Julia.

"I think I can vouch for all of us, Julia, we didn't sleep very well. Can you unravel these cases for us?" asks Bobbie.

"Well, what we have now is a deceased Barbara, a nymphomaniac and her brother Johnny, a split personality type, who orchestrated all of this. Samantha, the wife of Mark, called in the first missing person. Mark was abducted by Johnny and dragged to the school basement.

Barbara was having an affair with Mark. She was a friend of Samantha's. When Barbara got sick of one man, being Mark, it was time for another. Samantha found out that Mark was having an affair with Barbara, and when Barbara realized Samantha knew, she killed Samantha by strangulation. The body has yet to be found," says Julia.

"How did you get these details, Julia?" asks Bobbie.

"I did get a confession from Johnny, and Amanda's DNA sampling proved it. Johnny had to do away with Mark due to Barbara's request. Johnny, being the split personality type, presumably tortured Mark in the school basement until he finally killed him by burning him until his head was severed. Barbara and Johnny then fled due to thinking they may be found out. So, they ended up in Stanton County to set up the next missing persons case. It appears that Barbara lassoed Lewis into the Banjos Diner. You see, Barbara's affliction made her indulge in sexual relations, but this indulgence had to happen on a very regular basis. Lewis was her next target. She made it look like he lifted her dress when trying to retrieve her purse, which she purposely dropped to get him detained by a police officer. You guessed it, and the police officer was Johnny with one of his personalities. Barbara knew she could not get Lewis to her home, so she got Lewis in the alley while Johnny held him down. She raped Lewis there in the alley, thus the Coroner's report indicating Lewis having semen on him and his clothes. Johnny, the Executioner, then, had to dispose of Lewis. You see, Johnny not only had a split personality for many types of people, but he also had a personality of being a person of torture. According to the Coroner's report, Lewis's head was severed by a continual slamming of the lid to the dumpster, on his neck. One thing Barbara and Johnny forgot about is Lewis's cell phone in his pocket. If it wasn't for that, we might not have figured this whole thing out," says Julia.

"What I don't understand is why Johnny, or Judge Masters and then the Executioner, changed from executing me to executing his sister," says Richard.

"I can make a guess, Richard," says Amanda.

"So can I, Amanda," says Bobbie.

"You see Richard, a nymphomaniac must have sex very regularly, just like needing food every day, except worse. Barbara's appetite for sex could not be satiated enough due to not having enough men to have sex with," says Amanda.

"Yeah, but why didn't Barbara just keep Lewis around for all of the sex she needed?" asks Richard.

"Because, Richard, she not only needed sex regularly but needed variety to satisfy her indulgence totally," says Bobbie.

"Well…"

"Save it, Richard! Let Amanda finish," says Bobbie.

"It appears because of Johnny's reaction to Barbara, in the end, as you all witnessed, she was forcibly making Johnny have sex with her. I tested the semen on the bed sheets to Johnny's semen on his underwear, and there was a match. I also have the report from the Coroner that shows Johnny's semen on Barbara's leg, obviously coming from ejaculation within Barbara," explains Amanda.

"Ewe, yuck! Didn't she ever wash down there?" asks Richard.

"A woman of that type of affliction finds it hard to keep herself clean down there. I assume she must have forced Johnny into sex earlier in the day," says Julia.

"Well, I consider myself a nymphomaniac, but I am satisfied with just one woman," boasts Richard.

"We know that, Richard," says Bobbie, Amanda, and Julia in unison.

"Julia, what will become of Johnny?" asks Bobbie.

"Well, he will live out his murder charges in the Mental Institution. I believe in a short time he will get stuck in a personality that excludes all he did," says Julia.

"So, what about Ronald Tier, Julia?" asks Richard.

"He will never get out. They put him in a Mental Institution as well. That guy just mumbles nonsense," says Julia.

"Well, Julia, what is next?" asks Bobbie.

"The phone is quiet; the city of Harford is quiet. Let's take a trip over to Banjos and have lunch," suggests Julia.

"Let's not, Julia. I can't get that scene out of my mind," says Richard.

"Yeah, I bet Richard. We still need to talk about that!" exclaims Bobbie.

"Bobbie, honey, I didn't do anything, I swear. She did all of it!" exclaims Richard.

"Well, you did take her up on the invite for tea," says Bobbie.

"I, I, I…had a hunch! You know, like Julia's hunches," says Richard.

"OK, Richard. The only way you will get off from this is to make it up to me," says Bobbie.

"No problem, sweetheart! I feel my nymphomaniac personality kicking in," says Richard.

"Oh, brother! Here we go again!" exclaims Julia.

"Can we at least call for a take-out lunch before you two slip into sexual bliss?" asks Amanda.

BONNIE - SIX MONTHS LATER

"Hey, mister! What are you doing here on a night like this, raining and all?" asks Bonnie.

"I frequent this bar most nights," answers Ray.

"What about your family, Ray? Don't they wonder where you are?"

"No, I don't have a family. I just have a wife, or at least that is what I should call her."

"What do you mean, Ray? You and your wife not getting along?"

"I just as soon not discuss it. I don't even know why I am talking to you. I am finished with women!"

"Oh, Ray, I am sorry to hear that. Is there something I could do to ease your pain?"

"Oh, I don't know...what did you say your name was?"

"My name is Bonnie. Do you know something, Ray? It is a cold and rainy night. How about we go somewhere and warm up. I might be able to soothe your woes at the same time."

"I don't know...where would we go?"

"Tell you what. Do you have a car? I walked here and now that it is raining..."

"Yes, I have a car."

"Good, let's say you and I drive around a little bit. Does that sound like a good idea to you, Ray?"

"Well, I guess so, but don't expect much from me. As I told you, I am through with women."

"Let me see if I can help you with that feeling," says Bonnie.

———

"Ray, would you like to stop in at my apartment to have a warm cup of tea or hot chocolate?" asks Bonnie.

"Well, I shouldn't. I already told you I was through with women."

"Ray, I am only asking you if you would like some warm refreshment. My apartment is in the next block."

"OK, but I will not be able to stay very long."

"Go ahead, Ray, and have a seat on the couch. What would you like, tea or hot chocolate?"

"Tea would be fine, Bonnie."

"So, Ray, you were starting to tell me about the reasons what you are turned off by women or a woman in your case."

"My wife, she just vegetates in front of the television and ignores me. I try to strike up a conversation with her, but she just tells me to be quiet so she can hear the show she is watching."

"So she is inattentive…"

"She won't touch me. We haven't had sex since our honeymoon twenty years ago."

"Why, what happened, Ray?"

"I don't honestly know."

"So what do you do…….you know, about your desires, urges?"

"I go to the bar and drink myself numb."

"Does that work for you, Ray?"

"I don't know, I just…"

"Tell you what. You just stay seated, and I will be right back."

"Maybe I should go," states Ray

"No, I will be right back."

JESSICA

"Who are you, and what are you doing?" asks Ray.

"My name is Jessica, and I am here to keep you company."

"Where is Bonnie? She told me to sit here until she returns."

"Bonnie? Oh, her? She had to go to work and told me to keep you company."

"I don't think I like this. You appear to me to be a hooker of some sort."

"Why? You don't like my outfit?"

"What outfit? I don't call that clothing you are wearing…"

"What is the matter, Ray? Haven't you seen a woman in stretch type clothing?"

"Well, not lately. I can see that…"

"You can see what Ray? Do my erect nipples turn you off? How about this down here? Take a look at my crotch. Do you like what you see? Here, I will come closer."

"No, No, that is far enough!"

"Look, Ray, I bet you thought that was part of my pants, but guess what…yup, there is no cloth covering my crotch. What you see are my pubes."

"I don't like this…what is your name?"

"Jessica."

"Jessica, I don't like this one bit…"

"Listen, you bastard! You are going to like this, so just shut your mouth and get ready!"

"Ready for what?"

"See this knife? You are going to do exactly what I tell you."

"I need to go!"

"Shut up and remove your pants! Now put your arms behind your back and hold your feet together."

"What are you going to do to me?"

"Once I get your hands and feet tied, I will show you."

"I will yell if you touch me down there," says Ray.

"OK, I was hoping I didn't have to place a gag in your mouth. I want to hear you moan. It is all part of the ritual, you know."

"What rit…?"

"There, now I can do my job. That didn't take very long, and you said you didn't like what you see?"

Ray starts to squirm on the couch as Jessica places her hand around his cock and starts stroking its shaft.

"Stop moving! Yeah, just like that. How does it feel Ray, to have my pussy engulf you? I don't even need to take my pants off. Now be still as you can," says Jessica while she straddles Rays lap and settles herself on his cock.

"Get off of me, you bitch!" exclaims Ray in a baffled voice.

"Now look, Ray, it appears you have been taking some sort of pills for sustained erection. I have been stroking your cock for some time, and even though you have ejaculated, you still are as stiff as when we started. I know you can't answer that, all gagged up and all, but I am just going to keep bouncing away on your lap while I finger my clit for my ecstasy moments," says Jessica.

JIMMY

"OK, Ray, I have had enough orgasms, and I am kind of sick of hopping up and down on your penis. I am going into the bathroom to take a shower. Thanks for the enjoyment. I hope you enjoyed it as much as I have."

"Jessica, did you have to do that again? You know what that means and what I have to do now."

"Jimmy, you know I needed to have sex tonight! I didn't hurt him, and I thought I was gentle with him, although I feel a little chafed in my pussy."

"You didn't have to ride him so much, did you, Jessica?"

"Look, I don't tell you what to do, so don't you be telling me what I can or cannot do. Jimmy, what are you going to do now? What is the method?"

"I will take him across town and dump him in the alley."

"Why must you always have to dispose of my sex partners?"

"Sex partners? You mean the guys you rape!"

"Come on, Jimmy. I don't rape my men. They all want it and ask for it."

"Oh, really! How did he ask for it?"

"He told me he couldn't get it from his woman, so I obliged him."

"Yeah, and I have to get rid of him, so you don't get caught. No traces."

"Jimmy, I wish you weren't my brother because I have a hankering to fuck you."

"Jessica, we have been over that numerous times. You go fuck someone else and never me."

AN EXPLANATION

The gag is removed from Ray's mouth, and he starts to cough as he gasps for air.

"Who the hell are you?" asks Ray of the person who is standing in front of him.

"My name is Jimmy. Jessica told me she is done fucking you and turned you over to me."

"Where is Jessica? You look…….," questions Ray.

"Oh, she had to leave after her shower. I believe she muttered she had another man to meet."

"What the hell is going on here, anyway?" asks Ray in disbelief.

"Simple! Bonnie picked you up at the bar and brought you here. When you told her how you hadn't been fucked for twenty some odd years, she introduces Jessica, who is a streetwalker, so they call themselves, to fuck you. Now that it is over, she has sent me to take you back to the bar or your home. It is as easy as that. You can go on your merry way now and won't ever see any of us again. I sure hope you didn't catch anything from that snatch of Jessica's'. You know what they say about whores. They can easily fuck ten men or women, for that fact, a night."

"I am going to have to go to the authorities about what happened here. My wife will be worried about me as to why I am late getting home," says Ray.

"From what I hear, your wife doesn't pay attention to you, so I don't think she is missing you at the moment," says Jimmy.

"You won't get away with this!" exclaims Ray.

"What are you going to tell the authorities? They are pretty used to what the whores around here are doing. As a matter of fact, I know a few officers that frequent Jessica and the others quite regularly," says Jimmy.

"Untie me and give me my pants. I want you to take me to my home and not the bar," states Ray.

LOSING YOUR HEAD

"Where are you taking me? I told you my address, and this is not the direction, and this is not the town," screams Ray.

"Shut up!"

"Who are you people?"

"What is that you say, Bonnie?" asks Jimmy.

"Jimmy, he is such a sweet man. Are you sure you want to do this?"

"Look, Bonnie, I already told you. Jessica fucked this guy, and she is afraid she will get in trouble. If she does get into trouble, it will trace back to you because you told Jessica to go and fuck him," states Jimmy.

"Why did you ask me to come along with you Jimmy?" asks Bonnie.

"I will need your help when I get there," says Jimmy.

"Help for what and get where?" asks Ray.

"Ray, honey, did Jessica take care of you just the way you would have liked?" asks Bonnie.

"What the hell is this!" exclaims Ray.

"Here we are," says Jimmy.

"What are we doing in this alley? What are you crazy people doing?" asks Ray excitedly.

53

"Bonnie, put this gag in his mouth and help me lift him here," says Jimmy.

"Let me go! Let me go!" exclaims Ray.

"Hang on to him, Bonnie. I need to quiet him down," says Jimmy.

"Jimmy, did you have to hit him that hard? Now he is unconscious," says Bonnie.

"Just help me hoist him up on the dumpster. Now you hold him there while I slam the cover down," says Jimmy.

"Jimmy, stop it! You are going to kill him!" exclaims Bonnie.

"Whoops, I guess I slammed the cover too many times. His head just fell off of his neck. Poor devil," says Jimmy.

"Jimmy, I need to find another man tomorrow night," says Jessica.

"Why don't you just keep those guys instead of having me take care of them?" asks Jimmy.

"I wouldn't have to search them out if you would let me fuck you!"

"I told you, Jessica, it ain't ever going to happen!"

"Fine, I will continue to get bored and have you take care of them when I am finished with them," says Jessica.

THE PRESCRIPTION

"Bonnie?"

    "Yes, Jessica, what is it?"

"Did you get my prescription from the pharmacy? I am running out," says Jessica.

"Jessica don't use so much. That stuff is tough to have made," says Bonnie.

"OK, OK," says Jessica.

THE BABY BUMP AND THE GOD MOTHER

"Julia, did Betsy get a hold of you?" asks Bobbie.

"Oh, she might have tried, but I was in the shower. Although I don't see a message on my phone."

"What time will you be in the office, Julia?"

"I should be there in about an hour. I have to get my run in."

"Oh, I wish I could join you, but I feel and look like a beached whale," says Bobbie.

"Are you sure you aren't having twins, Bobbie?"

"The doctor says she can hear only one heartbeat, and the sonogram only shows one baby."

"Is there anything urgent I need to know about, Bobbie?"

"Well, yes, but it can wait until you get in the office. Have a great run, and I will miss you. By the way, once I deliver this bundle of joy that Richard gave me, I want to join you at the gym and continue our workouts together again," says Bobbie.

"That would be splendid, Bobbie. It is amazing that even though I am getting older, guys at the gym still stare at me and try to get me to go out with them. Just the other day, a guy at the gym ran into me from behind, by mistake, so he says, and as he was apologizing, I swear he brushed my bottom with the front of his hand and as he removed it he curved it inward towards my crotch."

"Oh my, Julia, what did you say to him?"

"I didn't say anything. I just walked away as visions of Ron flashed in my mind."

"Yeah, Ron! He certainly was a sleaze bag."

"Well, it just goes to show you, Julia, you will be propositioned well into your eighties," Bobbie says laughingly.

"Watch it, girl! You will be in the same boat, you vixen."

"With Richard around, I probably will still be having babies when I am eighty," says Bobbie in a jokingly manner.

"Listen, lady, I can't handle a busload of godchildren," says Julia.

"Ha, Ha! Anyway, enjoy your run, and I will see you at the office," says Bobbie.

"Hi, Amanda and Angela! It sure is nice to see you two working together. Angela, you are looking gorgeous today," remarks Bobbie.

"You can say that again, Bobbie," says Richard as he enters from within the conference room.

"How did you beat me here, Richard? Furthermore, stop trying to flirt with Angela!" exclaims Bobbie.

"Oh, I was just friendly, my love. I sneaked out of the house while you were showering. I had to bring the squad car back, and I also was looking at the news on the PC," says Richard.

"I can't wait for Julia to show up. There is something bizarre going on in Harford again," says Bobbie.

"Richard! Stop it! Not in front of these two gals! Oh!" exclaims Bobbie.

"I am not ashamed to show how much I love you, sweetheart, and that kiss proves it."

"Yeah, well, what did that slap on my butt signify?"

"Oh, just a gentle reminder that you are the girl for me."

"I think it shows Richard. In case you didn't notice, but I have this huge problem in the front of me, and it is your doing," says Bobbie.

"Baby in the oven," says Richard as he walks back into the conference room.

"You two are quite the pair. I love watching you two interact together. You have a very healthy marriage, Bobbie," says Amanda.

"Yes, and I have three very healthy girls and another on the way to prove it," says Bobbie.

"When are you due, Bobbie?" asks Angela.

"I feel like I could go into labor right now. I have about two months to go, maybe," answers Bobbie.

"Hey, Julia, how was your run this morning?" asks Amanda.

"It was very stimulating, and I met this most interesting dog while I was running. The dog wanted to run with me and was not paying attention to his owner. Unfortunately for me, the owner of the dog was a male of about in his mid-sixties, and you know I became the center of attention when I stopped to pet the dog."

"So, did he ask you for a date?" asks Bobbie.

"Very funny, girl! His eyes asked me for a date," says Julia.

"Julia, can we assemble in the conference room? Richard is already in there," says Bobbie.

ANGELA FITS IN

"So what do we have going on, Bobble?" asks Julia.

"Well, you see, there was a dead body found in a dumpster on Third Street over in Hannibal behind a bar. The strange thing is the body was decapitated just like the 'Johnny' case we just unraveled," says Bobbie.

"Interesting! Do the authorities over there want us to intervene?" asks Julia.

"I asked Betsy that when she got off of the phone and she stated that they didn't need us quite yet," says Amanda.

"OK, I will still catch up with them and get some statistics and facts just in case we are needed. Angela, please set up a file for me. Label it 'Unknown Body in a Dumpster-Hannibal'. As soon as I get some information, I will get back in touch with you to enter it into the system," says Julia.

"Sounds good, Julia," says Angela.

SEX AND THE DUMPSTER

"Angela, here is the information I need you to enter into the database for the unknown victim in the dumpster in Hannibal. The Coroner said the body was a male in his middle fifties. His head was taken from his body by way of slamming the dumpster cover on his neck. The victim had remnants of semen and vaginal fluid on his penis. It appears he had sex before he was brought to the dumpster. There were remnants of black pubic hair also sticking to his penis and his thighs. He also had traces of some chemicals in his blood for sustained erections. His wrists and ankles appeared to have been tied with some sort of rope. Both thighs had slight bruising as if someone of something was hitting them. My assumption, just because of what I have been told here, the victim was sitting, while whomever, I assume a female, performed sex on his erected penis while she bounced on his lap," says Julia.

"Having sex in that position would cause bruising?" asks Angela.

"All I can say is that she must have been riding him very hard and very long," responds Julia.

MIMIC?

"Julia, this is starting to mimic the case we just closed with Barbara and Johnny," states Richard.

"What are the chances that the same type of crime is happening again," says Bobbie.

"We will wait and see what transpires. I have a hunch we will have to take over for the locals over there. This case will probably get broader than what they can or want to handle. I am just waiting for the call," says Julia.

JULIA TAKES THE CASE

"What is it, Betsy?" asks Julia.

"Chief Ronald over in Hannibal would like to speak to you."

"OK, Betsy, patch him through."

"Chief Ms. Julia Lillus, this is Chief Ronald over at the Hannibal Police Department."

"This is Julia. You needn't be so formal; Julia will do just fine."

"OK, Julia, you know about the dumpster murder we have over here? I believe one of my officers has clued you in on the facts and statistics?"

"Yes, I have started a file."

"Julia, we would like your Department to handle this case. We don't have the Forensic expertise you have, and the town wants us to handle small-town stuff. They have also contacted your Council, and they have approved it."

"We can certainly help you with this case," says Julia.

"Julia, we will be giving the case directly over to you. We won't be able to handle any of it."

"Chief Ronald, I understand, but out of common courteous, will it be all right if I at least keep you abreast of what is going on?"

"Sure, and if more of it becomes apparent, I will be the first to call you."

"That sounds like a plan, Chief Ronald," states Julia.

THE DEPARTMENT IS DISPATCHED

"Amanda, go down to the Coroner's office and request DNA samples of the substances on the victim's penis and his cheek. Also, take samples of what is under his fingernails in case he scratched the person he may have had forced sex or the Executioner. Take Angela with you. She needs to see how we work," says Julia.

"OK, Julia, I will test the samples and log the data into the database. What will our next move be?" asks Amanda.

"Richard, I want you to do your typical and go over to Hannibal and snoop around and see if anyone had seen anything that might give us a clue of what happened and by whom," says Julia.

"What would you like me to do, Julia?" asks Bobbie.

"You, young lady! I want you to sit down and take a load off of your feet. You are so, well, bumped out to be wandering the streets. There will be plenty for you to do here in the office, as soon as we get more information," says Julia.

WHERE WAS IT DONE?

"Julia, no one seems to know anything about the murder in Hannibal. They didn't see or hear anything," says Richard.

"I wonder where the sex act was performed. I am sure it wasn't in the alley," says Julia.

"I think we need to survey the outskirts of the village," says Bobbie.

"Amanda and Angela, please go to the village of Clarion and see if anything unusual was seen or heard by the residents. I would start in bars," says Julia.

"I will scour the village of Banton," says Richard.

"Great! Keep me posted. Your wife and I must leave for the birthing coach class," says Julia.

ROGER

"Hey honey, what's a girl like you doing in a place like this?"

"Hey sugar, I come here often. I am considered the 'mother' of this here, bar," says Bonnie.

"What do you mean by 'mother.'"

"Well, you see, I sit here at the bar, and guys come over and talk to me about their problems. I listen and offer some suggestions," says Bonnie.

"Well, I am looking for some action tonight."

"Action!" exclaims Bonnie.

"Yeah, you know. I want some pussy tonight. Do you think you can help me with my problem?"

"What a coincidence I happen to know a gal, who can help you," says Bonnie.

"I was hoping you were up to it."

"No, 'mother' doesn't do that, but I do have a resource for you if you would like to drive me home. I can arrange for you to meet her. Her name is Jessica," says Bonnie.

"Sure, maybe by then you will change your mind. You look like a gal who needs a good fuck, and I am the one who can do it!"

"Keep it in your pants, sir! Let's get going," says Bonnie.

"Here is my apartment. Let me call Jessica and have her come over," says Bonnie.

"Hello, my name is Jessica, and what is your name, lover boy?"

"My name is Roger. Where is Bonnie?"

"Oh, she left. She doesn't like to watch," says Jessica.

"I wanted to talk her into a twosome."

"Roger, I am all the pussy you need! I don't want to hear about Bonnie again! Do you understand?"

"Well, yes. You don't have to be so touchy. Now how do you want it?"

"Roger, you don't run the show. I do, now get on the bed and lie down!"

"Let me see those tits and let me suck those nipples of yours. That will get me hard," says Roger.

"No! You will get hard if I slap it a few times."

"What kind of whore are you, Jessica? All the whores I have fucked always let me suck their nipples, and they have never slapped my cock to get it hard."

"Look, are you going to get hard or not?" asks Jessica.

"Not by the method you are using!"

"I got to go pee. You had better be hard by the time I get back," says Jessica.

"Oh no, you don't! Get your ass over here and spread those legs! Bonnie promised she could cure my problem, and you are it!"

"You had better let go of me, Roger!"

"No! Now you just get on your hands and knees while I stick my fingers into your pussy to get it wet."

"Jimmy! Jimmy! Please get in here and help me!" exclaims Jessica.

"See, you juice up just fine," says Roger as he slips his fingers into her.

"Now, you get in there and pee! I expect you to get back out here, and I will straddle you. Fat chance you are calling the shots, bitch!"

"Who the hell are you, and where is Jessica?" asks Roger.

I am Jimmy, Jessica's brother, and she summoned me for help. I understand you want to be in charge. My sister doesn't like that. She is always in charge," says Jimmy.

"What is that you say, Jessica?" asks Jimmy.

"What the hell! What the hell are you?" asks Roger.

"Jessica wants me to slit your throat, and that is what I am going to do!" exclaims Jimmy.

"Get away from me, you, you,......," screams Roger just as Jimmy's knife slices a gash into Roger's arm.

The next plunge that Jimmy makes towards Roger makes its mark as the knife goes clean across Roger's throat. Roger sees a flash of light, and then everything goes dark as he hits the floor.

"There, Jessica, I did it. I hope you are happy now," says Jimmy.

"I didn't get a fuck out of him. I am desperate now! Go get someone; any male you can find out there in the street. I need to get laid tonight...unless you want to do the favor, Jimmy."

"Shut the fuck up, Jessica! I will tell Bonnie you are a bad girl," says Jimmy.

"What's wrong, Jimmy?" asks Bonnie.

"Jessica is trying to get me to fuck her, and I won't do it!" exclaims Jimmy.

"Jessica, you leave Jimmy alone. If he doesn't want to fuck you, then he doesn't want to fuck you," says Bonnie.

'What do we do with the body Bonnie?" asks Jimmy.

"We can't take it across town. It is too late, and someone will see us. Go back to the bar and drop him in the dumpster in the alley," says Bonnie.

"Bonnie, you are getting lazy. Jimmy is going to get caught," states Jessica.

"Jessica, you stay out of this! Your job is to satisfy the gentlemen I bring to you. I handle the rest," says Bonnie.

THE CORONER

"Julia, we just received a call from the local sheriff in Clark County. It seems they have found a body in a dumpster outside a bar called the Thirsty Traveler. This body is a male and has had his throat cut," says Bobbie.

"Richard, get over to Clark County and go to the Thirsty Traveler and see if anyone knows anything. I am going over to the Coroner's Office and see what his first takes are on this body. Amanda, while I am there, I will request DNA tests. As soon as I clear it with the Coroner, I will have you go and collect samples. Collect the same type of samples you did with the other dumpster case," says Julia.

"Hello, my name is Chief Julia Lillus from the Harford Police Department, and we...

"Yes, I have been waiting for you. Here is the rundown. The victim is a male in his middle fifties and has had his throat slit," says the Coroner.

"Did you happen to find anything else strange on the body?" asks Julia.

"Well, I don't know how it could be related, but the gentleman has some slight abrasions on his penis. My tests also detected semen," says the Coroner.

"OK, maybe he was having a hard time relieving himself," states Julia.

"There appears to have been a female involved, though. I found some black pubic hair stuck on the film of semen. There also appears to have a substance on him which resembles vaginal discharge on his penis and his thighs."

"Would it be OK if I send my Forensic Examiner over to collect DNA samples?" asks Julia.

"Sure, I was given specific instructions to cooperate with you and your Police Department," says the Coroner.

"Thank you, and I will send her over later this afternoon. Her name is Amanda and her technician Angela," says Julia.

SARA

"Hello, my name is Officer Richard Peltz from the Harford Police Department. Who are you?"

"My name is Sara."

"Sara, do you work the bar much of the time?"

"Yes, they kind of use me as the manager at the Thirsty Traveler."

"I am here because of a supposed murder that occurred outside this establishment."

"Yeah, they found a guy in the dumpster in the alley."

"Sara, was there any commotion or disturbance a couple of nights ago?" asks Richard.

"No, not really, but there was a guy in here Wednesday night trying to 'hit' on me," says Sara.

"What happened?" asks Richard.

"About the time I made my point that I wasn't interested, a strange-looking woman came in and settled herself right next to this guy."

"What happened then?"

"They started in some small talk, and I heard some of their conversations. He was 'hitting' on her and wanted to have sex with her."

"Did she take him up on it, Sara? And about what time was it when this was happening?"

"They left together. I really do not remember the time," says Sara.

"Sara, would you come with me to my office and look at a picture we have, to possibly make an identification?" asks Richard.

"Sure, give me about thirty minutes, and I will be off my shift."

"Julia, this is Sara. She is the bartender at the Thirsty Traveler. I would like her to look at the picture of our latest victim," says Richard.

"Hi, Sara. My name is Julia Lillus, and I am the Chief here at this Police Department. Take a look at this picture."

"Is that the murder victim found outside the bar?" asks Sara.

"Yes, it is. Does he look familiar to you?" asks Richard.

"Yes! Officer Peltz, that is the guy I was telling you about who was trying to 'hit' on me and then that woman," says Sara.

"What woman was that, Sara?" asks Julia.

"She was the strangest looking thing. She was engaging in small talk with him at the bar, and they left together after he pestered her for sex," says Sara.

"I see. We will take you back to the Thirsty Traveler. We appreciate you coming here for identification purposes," says Julia.

"I will take her back, Julia," says Bobbie.

"Did you get Sara back to the Thirsty Traveler with no problems, Bobbie?" asks Julia.

"Yes, there was no way I was going to let Richard take her back! Did you notice the clothes she was wearing? There was no need to fantasize. All of her female traits were very visible. No need for imagination. And she was probably not much older than twenty-two years in age," says Bobbie.

"I guess that is the type of attire one wears when tending a bar. I guess it brings customers in," says Julia.

"She wonders why that guy was hitting on her," says Bobbie.

"Richard, I want you to visit the Thirsty Traveler for a couple of nights this week. I have a hunch this woman has something to do with this case and maybe even the previous dumpster case," says Julia.

"Richard, I don't want you carrying on with that Sara when you are there," states Bobbie.

"Don't worry, babe, you are my type and she certainly is not mine," says Richard.

"Well, don't go staring at her female-wares," says Bobbie.

"Hi, Officer Peltz! What brings you here?" asks Sara.

"Police work. I am hoping that woman shows up here. We think she might be in this area. Whatever you do, don't let on to anyone you know me," says Richard.

"I won't," says Sara.

BONNIE INTERVIEWS RICHARD

"Hey, you, bartender. Have you seen that guy I was with the other night?" asks Bonnie.

"No, I don't pay attention to who comes and goes at this establishment," says Sara.

"Well, I had him take me home, and he dropped me off. He didn't even want to come in with me. He was so hot to get into my pants, and then he went cold. What do you think about that, girl?" asks Bonnie.

"I don't get into anybody's business. Do you want a drink?" asks Sara.

"Hey, what is with that guy over there? He is quite the handsome type," says Bonnie.

"Hey, mister! Do you want to have a drink with me?" asks Bonnie.

"No, I am OK, " answers Richard.

"So, what is a handsome guy like you doing in a bar like this?" asks Bonnie.

"I guess I should ask you the same," says Richard.

"Do you mind if I have a seat, here, with you? We can chat some," says Bonnie.

"Be my guest," says Richard.

"Are you married, mister?" asks Bonnie.

"Yes, I am. I have a beautiful wife and three adorable girls and another baby on the way," answers Richard.

"My, my, you certainly have been busy keeping your wife on her back with her legs spread," says Bonnie.

"Listen, what do you want to talk to me about other than my personal life?" asks Richard.

"You see, I help guys in need of advice with their problems," says Bonnie.

"I don't have any problems needing your advice," says Richard.

"I was thinking, you being a man with such a large family, might have difficulties servicing his wife while not getting her pregnant again," says Bonnie.

"I have no problems in that area," says Richard.

"What if I told you I have an excellent friend who is very knowledgeable in satisfying men. She can give you a night of total bliss. You won't have to think about pregnancy; you can pleasure yourself with no holding back. I promise she can give you sex as you have never had it before," says Bonnie.

"No, thanks. My wife satisfies me and I am in no need of sex with another female," says Richard.

"It seems to have started raining. Do you think you could drive me to my apartment?" asks Bonnie.

"I guess I could do that, but I don't want the help of your friend," says Richard.

"Oh no, she won't be there," says Bonnie.

"Would you please see me in? I am afraid to enter my apartment alone," Bonnie requests.

"All right, I will be leaving now," says Richard.

"Wait just a minute while I get some lights on," says Bonnie.

"Well, who do we have here?"

"Who are you?" asks Richard.

"My name is Jessica, and I am here to ease your stress," says Jessica.

"I don't have any stress, and where is the woman I brought here?" asks Richard.

"Oh, she is somewhere, I am sure. I understand you are quite busy with your wife making children," states Jessica.

"I am going to leave now," says Richard.

"Jimmy, could you come out here for a minute?" asks Jessica.

"What is it, Jessica?" asks Jimmy.

"This guy isn't cooperating. He is unwilling to fuck me!" exclaims Jessica.

"Wait just a minute! What is going on here?" asks Richard.

"You need to fuck me," states Jessica.

"Listen, mister! If you don't satisfy Jessica, she will have have me take care of you," says Jimmy.

"And just what does that mean?" asks Richard.

"I dumped a couple of guys in a dumpster after she fucked them. I don't know what she will want if you refuse to fuck her," says Jimmy.

"Alright, whoever you are. My name is Officer Richard Peltz, and I am arresting you for the recent murder of a victim loaded into a dumpster in the alley behind the Thirsty Traveler Bar. You have the right to remain silent. Anything you say can and will be used against you in the court of law," states Richard.

BIZARRE EXPLANATION

"OK, guys, meet me in the conference room in about five minutes," says Julia.

"I hope it is about this strange case, or cases, I should say," says Bobbie.

"Let me give you a rundown of the most recent case of the dumpster murder. Richard, I will have you start, seeing you interacted with the murderers," says Julia.

"The murder was completed by one person...one person with three different personalities. I experienced a woman who goes by the name of Bonnie. She is kind of a preliminary interviewer to coerce males into her apartment. Once there, Jessica takes over, and she is the one who forces sex with the male. Once she is finished with her desires, Jimmy is summoned to dispose of the male after he is murdered in some fashion. In this case, slitting his throat and dumping him in a dumpster," says Richard.

"So, how did this Jimmy, being a female able to lift a dead body all by herself to put the victim in a dumpster," asks Angela.

"Bonnie, Jessica, and Jimmy is a transgender person who started as a male by birth," says Richard.

"That explains the strength issue," says Angela.

"Amanda's DNA testing proves Jessica was the one who had sex with our victim. The confusing thing, Amanda, is your report states the matching of semen, but what about the vaginal fluid you found?" asks Julia.

"Well, you all may not be able to understand this, but in that Jessica is a transgender person, he had the operation to replace his penis with a vagina. In no way to recreate vaginal fluid, they found a way to have a lubricant made so close to the chemical makeup of actual vaginal fluid that it took scrutiny to see there was a difference chemically. I am not sure why she had to have that. Any vaginal lubricant would have worked," says Amanda.

"So, she had to insert this fluid into her vagina before having sex with the victim?" asks Richard.

"Yes, Richard!" exclaims Bobbie.

"I am a bit confused here. I was reading the notes to the case and there is mention Jimmy complained that Barbara often requested to have sex with him, and at times, did have sex with Barbara without his consent. How can that be when he had his penis removed and a vagina grafted on?" asks Angela.

"They found in his or her apartment an artificial penis that could be inserted in his new vagina. I assume it was made by the same people who crafted the artificial vaginal lubrication because it had the ability to emit a fluid when squeezed," says Julia.

"But how were these sexual acts all performed on one person? How did he or she reach an orgasm both as a male and a female?" asks Richard.

"I am thinking that the orgasms didn't happen as you or I would experience them. In some twisted way, depending on which role was in play, they didn't actually reach an orgasm physically, but mentally," answers Julia.

"This entire case baffles my mind," says Angela.

"I am so thankful for my honey, Bobbie, and her...er...I couldn't imagine not having a physical orgasm," says Richard.

"OK, enough of that. So why the sex serenade and then the murders?" asks Bobbie.

"That brings us back to the first dumpster murder with Barbara. Bonnie, Jessica, and Jimmy is the brother of Barbara. He has the same affliction for needing sex continuously as Barbara did. Jimmy is also suffering from split personalities. He/she had to murder his/her victim to suppress the victim, telling what had happened to them. Because of the need for sex, the pattern had to continue from victim to victim," says Julia.

"This is all so bazaar!" exclaims Bobbie.

"What is the 'cleanup' of this mess?" asks Richard.

"Bobbie, please go and visit the victims' family and tell them the sad news of their loss. I will clear up all details for Chief Ronald," says Julia.

"What happens to Bonnie, or is it Jessica? Jimmy?" asks Angela.

"They are headed to the Mental Institution in the prison. It is kind of interesting Bonnie told on Jessica and Jimmy by making a statement they were guilty of the murders," says Julia.

"Did she confess to all of the dumpster murders?" asks Angela.

"No, she did not. She placed the blame on the other two," says Julia.

"OK, that is over with, and the phone is quiet. It is Friday, and I want you all to take a three day weekend. I will see you all on Monday morning," says Julia.

"Julia, will you be available to watch our girls later this evening?" asks Bobbie.

"Certainly! I have a desire for mothering," says Julia.

Julia

Amanda

Angela

Bobbie

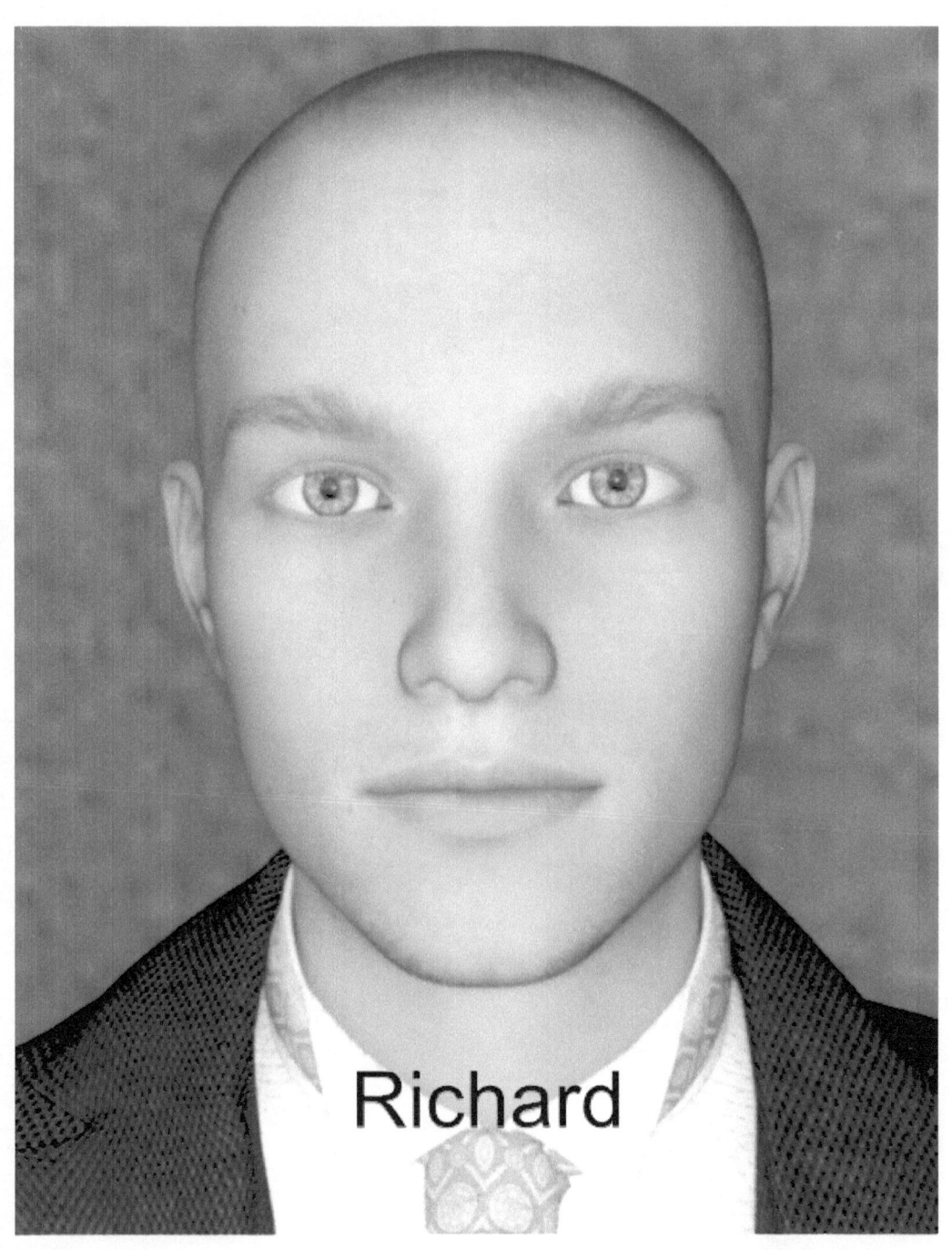

Richard

ABOUT THE AUTHOR

James Roberts, an emerging author of fictional Crime Thrillers, delivers to his readers the realization of twisted feelings, minds, and actions as well as true-to-life situations leading to criminal activities that are sometimes hard to fathom.

This book is James Robert's seventh.

www.ingramcontent.com/pod-product-compliance
Lightning Source LLC
Chambersburg PA
CBHW020632130626
46552CB00003B/1189